This
Treasure Cove Story
belongs to

I AM ANNA

A CENTUM BOOK 978-1-913865-27-6
Published in Great Britain by Centum Books Ltd.
This edition published 2021.

1 3 5 7 9 10 8 6 4 2

Centum Books Ltd, 20 Devon Square, Newton Abbot, Devon, TQ12 2HR, UK.
9/10 Fenian St, Dublin 2, D02 RX24, Ireland.

www.centumbooksltd.co.uk | books@centumbooksltd.co.uk
CENTUM BOOKS LIMITED. Reg. No. 07641486.

A CIP catalogue record for this book is available
from the British Library.

Printed in China.

DISNEY

FROZEN

I AM ANNA

By Christy Webster
Illustrated by Alan Batson

I am ANNA.

I live in the
kingdom of
ARENDELLE.

My sister, Elsa, and I were really
close when we were little.

We built a
snowman.

We went sledging.

We skated on the pond.

But one day she just
shut me out and I didn't
know why.

I spent my days talking to paintings.

It was lonely.

But then I found someone special.

Elsa wouldn't bless my marriage
to Hans because we'd just met...

that day.

I got mad,

she got upset . . .

...and her magic accidentally froze our **kingdom**!

She **RAN AWAY.**

I had to find her. I knew my sister
wouldn't hurt me.

And I was *born* ready for adventure.

On my search, I met new
friends – Kristoff, Sven and Olaf!

I found Elsa
on the North Mountain.

But she wanted to be alone.

Elsa didn't mean to do it,
but her magic froze my heart!

Kristoff took me to see
the trolls.

They told me that only an act of
true love can thaw a frozen heart.

We raced back to Hans.

But I was wrong about him. It wasn't true love.

Olaf helped me understand
what true *love* is.

I *love* my sister.

And my act of love for her thawed my heart.

As Olaf says… some people
are worth **melting** for.

Treasure Cove Stories

Please contact Centum Books
to receive the full list of titles in
the *Treasure Cove Stories* series.
books@centumbooksltd.co.uk

Book list may be subject to change. Not all titles are listed.